Bad Day for Badger

The Royal Society for the Prevention of Cruelty to Animals is the UK's largest animal charity. They rescue, look after and rehome hundreds of thousands of animals each year in England and Wales. They also offer advice on caring for all animals and campaign to change laws that will protect them. Their work relies on your support, and buying this book helps them save animals' lives.

www.rspca.org.uk

Bad Day for Badger

By Sarah Hawkins
Illustrated by Jon Davis

■SCHOLASTIC

First published in the UK in 2014 by Scholastic Children's Books
An imprint of Scholastic Ltd
Euston House, 24 Eversholt Street
London, NW1 1DB, UK
Registered office: Westfield Road, Southam, Warwickshire, CV47 0RA
SCHOLASTIC and associated logos are trademarks
and/or registered trademarks of Scholastic Inc.

ISBN 978 1407 13966 1

A CIP catalogue record for this book is available
from the British Library.

Printed and bound by CPI Group (UK) Ltd, Croydon, CR0 4YY
Papers used by Scholastic Children's Books are made
from wood grown in sustainable forests.

5 7 9 10 8 6

www.scholastic.co.uk

1

"So what game are we going to get, then?" Dad asked as they drove down the country lane into town.

"It's called *Ice Storm*," Lewis grinned. "I've played it round at Maddy's house and it's brilliant. You have to collect all these stars that give you superpowers, and the baddies throw icicles to try and freeze you."

Dad sighed. "I don't know why you don't do something useful, like read a book."

Lewis rolled his eyes. Whenever Mum had to go away to a sales conference, or

to visit Granny and Pops back in Jamaica,
he and Dad were stuck with each other all
weekend long. He loved his dad, but
all he ever did was work, and he seemed
to think that's all Lewis should do, too!
Yesterday, before she'd left, Mum had
suggested that they go into town and get
the game that Lewis had wanted for ages.
But Dad was even ruining that.

Lewis put his feet up on the car
dashboard and glanced at his dad. Dad

was long and lanky, like him, but that was about the only way that they looked the same. Lewis was like Mum, with chocolate-brown skin, dark eyes and afro hair. He liked wearing jeans and trainers, but Dad always wore smart clothes, even at the weekend. Dad's skin was white and freckly, and he had brown hair. Behind his sunglasses, Lewis knew that Dad had light blue eyes that twinkled when he smiled, but that didn't happen very often.

Dad glanced over at him. "Feet!" he warned Lewis immediately. Lewis gave an exaggerated sigh and put them down.

At least they were going to see Granddad tomorrow. Granddad was Dad's dad, and he was really fun. He was always telling Lewis exciting stories about his time in the Navy, or playing with Alfie, his old greyhound dog. Granddad was as fun as Dad was serious.

Sometimes Granddad seems like the young one, and Dad the grumpy old man! Lewis thought, grinning to himself.

He wound down the window as they drove down the little windy country lane, covered with fields on both sides. The sun was shining brightly, and the air smelled like cut grass and holidays. School was just about to start again, but it didn't really feel like autumn yet. Lewis had had a brilliant summer. He and Mum had gone to stay in Cornwall with his best friend Maddy and her family – her mum and her big brother Stephen. They'd been fishing and crabbing, and eaten ice cream every day. Dad hadn't come because he hadn't been able to take any time off from work.

Lewis stared out of the window as

he remembered his holiday. But as he was thinking, a flash of black and white caught his eye. Something was lying at the side of the road. "Dad, stop!" he said, sitting up in his seat and straining to look out of the window.

"What?" Dad quickly pulled the car over to the side of the road. "Are you OK?"

"I saw an animal," Lewis said, unbuckling his seat belt. "It was on the road, it might be hurt."

"Lewis, we can't just stop—" Dad began to say, but Lewis was already getting out of the car.

Making sure there was nothing coming, he ran across the lane. At the end of a row of parked cars, there was a small animal, lying very still.

Please let it be OK, Lewis thought as he

crept towards it. *Was it a cat, or a dog?* It had a dark grey body, and a stubby grey tail. As Lewis stepped closer, it looked up, and Lewis gasped as he saw its face. It had black and white lines over a long snuffly nose. Its eyes were black and beady, and it had little black paws, with strong-looking claws.

"It's a badger!" Lewis called excitedly to Dad in the car. "I've never seen one in real life before."

"It's probably got fleas," Dad called

back. "Come on."

"We can't just leave." Lewis stepped closer. The badger was only small, and its beady, black eyes looked up at him fearfully. As Lewis got closer, it shuffled backwards towards the nearest car, dragging one of its back legs behind it.

"Look, Dad, it *is* hurt," Lewis said. "We have to help."

"OK," Dad sighed and Lewis heard him getting out of the car. But the sound of the car door shutting startled the young badger. Before Lewis could move, it disappeared right underneath a van that was parked nearby.

"Oh no!" Lewis gasped. "She's scared." He kneeled down and peered under the van. The badger peeped back at him. "Don't be afraid," Lewis said. "We want to help you."

"Lewis, we can't stay here all day, or

you'll never get your game," Dad said. "She'll come out when she's ready. She's a wild animal, not a pet. And you don't even know if she's a girl, anyway."

"She looks like a girl. And I don't care about the game!" Lewis insisted. "There must be *something* we can do. What about the rescue centre where Granddad got Alfie? They help animals, don't they?"

"The RSPCA?" Dad said. "Actually, that's not a bad idea. Hold on, I'll give them a ring."

Dad walked back to the car and Lewis sighed with relief. "It's going to be OK," he promised the badger. She just peered up at him and snuffled her nose again.

Lewis looked around for something he could give her. He spotted a clump of grass and went and collected a handful.

"Come on, Badger," Lewis said

soothingly as he kneeled down and held a long blade of grass under the van. The badger's snout wriggled as she sniffed at it, but she didn't come out. "Come and get the nice food," Lewis coaxed her.

But the badger just stared at him. Lewis studied her face. He couldn't believe he was so close to a wild animal. Her eyes were bright and intelligent, like she understood every word he said. She had a dark nose, with fine, white whiskers poking out from either side. Her stripes were perfectly straight, like they'd been painted on. She was beautiful!

"Badgers don't eat grass," Dad told him as he reappeared with his phone. "They eat worms and snails, things like that."

"Oh," said Lewis, coming out from under the van and scrambling to his feet. "What did the RSPCA say?"

Dad held out his phone and showed him the RSPCA's website on the screen. "I rang the emergency hotline and they said they'll send an officer out straight away. There's a rescue centre just outside town. I didn't even know it was there."

"I knew they'd help!" Lewis said happily. He sat down again and, to his surprise, Dad kneeled down next to him. They both peered under the van. The badger looked back, curiously.

"I think I'll call her Bramble," Lewis said.

"Bramble?" Dad looked surprised. "That's a nice name. What made you think of that?"

Lewis smiled. "Granddad said that now it's September, it's almost time to go blackberry picking again. Last year Archie got stuck in a bramble bush. It took ages to get him out!"

Dad laughed and shook his head. "That dog is a troublemaker!"

Lewis glanced under the van. The badger looked back, her snuffly snout poking out.

"It's OK, Bramble," Lewis told the frightened badger. "Help will be here soon."

2

"Gotcha!" Dad laughed.

Lewis and Dad were playing a game on Dad's phone. Lewis couldn't believe how many games Dad had, and how good at them he was.

Dad had just beaten him for the fourth time when a white van drove down the road. Lewis spotted the blue RSPCA logo on the side and jumped up excitedly. "Careful," Dad said, as Lewis leaped into the middle of the road and started waving. "We don't want you getting injured, too."

The van carefully pulled up behind Dad's car, and a man got out. He had a short-sleeved white shirt with black flaps on the shoulders, a navy tie, and a black peaked cap. "Hello!" he called, taking off his sunglasses. "Did you phone about a badger?"

"Yes." Dad went over to shake the RSPCA officer's hand. "I'm Alex Riley," he told him.

"I'm Ray," the officer introduced himself.

"I'm Lewis, and the badger, she's called Bramble," Lewis said all in one breath.

"Oh, is she now?" Ray chuckled, his eyes twinkling. "What makes you so sure she's a girl? Expert in badgers, are we?" he joked.

"I've never actually seen one before," Lewis told him shyly. "But she just looks like a girl. I think she might be hurt."

Ray suddenly seemed serious. He opened the back of the RSPCA van and brought out a big wire carrier with a door at one end. "OK then. Let's take a look at her."

Lewis showed Ray the van, and they both looked under. For a second Lewis thought that Bramble had gone, but then he spotted her black beady eyes peering out nervously. She had squeezed even further back under the van, and had climbed up into the little space on top of the wheel.

"Hello, Bramble," Ray said softly. He turned to Lewis. "It looks like she's quite a young cub," he whispered. "I wonder what she's doing on her own. Usually cubs this small stay very close to the sett where they live."

Ray kneeled down, then lay flat. "I'm going to see if I can reach her," he told them as he started to wriggle right under the van.

"Cool!" Lewis grinned.

He went to follow Ray, but Dad stopped him. "Let him do his job," he said.

"You can hold my hat," Ray said,

appearing with a grin. He gave it to Lewis, then disappeared back under the van again. Lewis could hear his muffled voice as he spoke to Bramble. "What are you doing under there?" he asked. "Let's get you out and back to where you belong."

Lewis crouched down to watch. As Ray reached out, the little badger edged further and further up into the small gap above the wheel.

Ray stretched and reached out to Bramble, talking to her in a calm, low voice. But it was no good. Eventually he crawled out, shaking his head. He sat down and wiped the back of his hand over his face. "She's gone right up into the wheel suspension," he said with a frown.

Lewis peered under the van. Bramble was almost invisible, but he could just see her white stripes and the very tip of her snout.

"She probably likes the dark because badgers are nocturnal creatures," Ray said.

"What does that mean?" Lewis asked curiously.

"That's when something sleeps all day and only wakes up in the evening," Dad explained.

"Like Maddy's big brother!" Lewis joked. On holiday Stephen had spent all the time sleeping instead of doing anything fun.

Dad cracked a smile. "Yeah, all teenagers are a bit nocturnal!" he agreed.

Ray grinned, then went back to looking at the van, walking all round it, a thoughtful look on his face.

"Right," Dad said. "How are we going to get her out? I've got a jack in the boot of my car. We can use that to lift the van up. Maybe that'll help."

Ray looked at the van and shook his head. "I don't want to risk hurting her."

"She might come out if she's hungry," Lewis suggested. "I can go and look for some worms to feed her."

"I don't know about the worms, but food is a good plan," Ray agreed. "Maybe that will tempt her out. There are lots of things that we can feed badgers – they eat wet cat food, and some human food, too – apples, plums and even peanuts."

"I love peanuts!" Lewis grinned. "We don't have any in the car, though," he added, disappointedly.

"My lunch box is still in the car from yesterday," Dad said. "There might be some apple in there."

"I'll go and see!" Lewis volunteered. Dad threw him the keys, and he rushed over to the car and looked in the boot. Next to the spare tyre and jack, there was a torch and a first-aid kit, and Dad's work bag. Inside that was a lunch box with the leftovers from his packed lunch in it. Lewis gasped indignantly as he opened it. Dad had left the crusts of his sandwiches, even though he was always telling Lewis off for not eating his!

He moved the crusts and smiled as he

saw the crescents of apple Dad had left behind. They'd be perfect for Bramble.

Lewis picked them out of the lunch box, and grabbed the torch, too. He started to race back to the others, then slowed down to a walk. He wanted to run and shout, but he didn't want to scare Bramble. "I got this as well," he said, showing Dad and Ray the torch.

"Well done – I don't suppose you want a job with the RSPCA, do you?" Ray joked. "You're a natural."

Lewis grinned. He'd never have guessed that on his way into town he'd be having an adventure rescuing a badger! "Can I feed her?" he asked hopefully.

"I think I'd better do that," Ray told him. "She seems calm at the moment, but she is a wild animal, and they're unpredictable, especially when they're cornered like this. You can watch though."

"OK," Lewis agreed.

Ray wriggled back under the van and Lewis slipped down next to him. He watched excitedly as Ray held out the apple. Bramble's nose appeared, then her eyes as she reached her head out, stretching to get to the tasty treat.

"She's eating it!" Lewis whispered happily.

"Come on, Bramble, have some lovely apple," Ray said soothingly as he placed another bit of apple down, slightly out of her reach. Lewis could see what he was doing, leaving the apple like a trail to get her to come out of her hiding place. Ray moved backwards and Lewis shuffled after him, his trainers skidding on the road, until he was almost out from under the van. Ray put the next bit of apple down where Bramble could see it, then shuffled back even further.

Bramble's nose twitched as she smelled the food. Lewis and Ray stayed absolutely still, with just their heads looking under the van.

Bramble finished the first piece, and looked inquisitively at Lewis, her nose sniffing the air like she was asking for more. Her nose stretched even further out, then her stripy head followed. She stretched towards the apple – and stopped.

Ray tutted worriedly as he looked at her. "I think there might be a problem," he said. "Alex, can you pass me that torch?"

Dad's feet appeared, then his hand. When Dad shone the torch under the car, Bramble blinked unhappily and squirmed. But although she wriggled and twisted,

she couldn't get out from the space above the wheel. Bramble was stuck!

Ray got out from under the van, looking worried. "I just can't get far enough under to get her out," he explained.

Lewis looked at Bramble's confused little face. He didn't want to leave her. Above him, he could hear Ray radioing the RSPCA.

"We've got a problem here," Ray

3

"Here they are!" Ray called as a huge red engine appeared around the corner. Lewis felt a bit disappointed that it didn't have the blue lights flashing and the sirens going, but he guessed they didn't want to make Bramble the badger even more scared.

The fire engine stopped and four firefighters jumped out – three men and a lady. "I know we're supposed to rescue cats stuck up trees," the lady said as she came over to meet them, "but I've never heard of a badger being stuck under a van before!"

All four firefighters looked round the
van as Ray explained the situation. Lewis
watched in fascination. He hoped Bramble
wasn't too frightened. He could imagine
her under there, peering out at all the big
firefighters' boots and wondering what
was going to happen to her. She must be
really scared.

"I hear this is your badger, lad?" one of the firemen asked Lewis.

"Well, I found her. She's called Bramble," Lewis said shyly as he looked up at the big man. He was wearing a jacket and trousers with fluorescent shiny yellow stripes around the sleeves and legs, and a yellow hat.

"You can come and give me a hand then." He smiled. "I'm Chief Fire Officer Dorileo, but you can call me Antonio," he said with a wink.

Lewis followed the firefighter excitedly over to the big red fire engine. He'd never seen one up close before and it seemed so huge now he was standing next to it. It had a red front, with blue lights and ladders on top, and red and yellow squares painted on the back. Antonio pulled up a metal blind on the side of the engine.

Inside was a cupboard, with ropes and a hose all neatly curled and stored away.

Antonio saw him looking and nodded. "We've got all kinds of equipment, anything we might need in an emergency situation. And we have to be able to get to it really quickly. Your badger isn't in any danger at the moment, but sometimes it's life or death, so we have to move fast."

Lewis nodded.

"Every time we go back to the station we check all the equipment is in its place and ready to use," Antonio continued. "There's a lot of tidying up involved in being a firefighter!"

Lewis looked at all the kit curiously. "How are you going to get Bramble out?" he asked, staring at a huge circular saw.

Antonio caught him looking and
laughed. "We're not going to saw the van
in two just yet," he said. "First we'll see
if we can lift it up and get Bramble out
that way."

"Dad was going to use his car jack, but
Ray didn't want to hurt her," Lewis told
him anxiously.

"Our lifting bags have much more
control than a jack," Antonio told him.
"And we'll have Ray checking on her

welfare the whole way through. I promise your badger will be OK. Now, do you want to give me a hand with this?"

"Yes please!" Lewis breathed. As long as he knew Bramble would be all right, he could enjoy the adventure, helping out a real-life fireman!

Antonio gave Lewis some plastic squares to hold, then called over his team, and they all started working together. Lewis watched with interest as they brought lots of things out of the fire engine. There were some tubes, planks of wood and a big long container. *What were they going to do?*

Lewis watched as one of the firefighters went over to the van and started piling the wood next to the wheels, while the others quickly started setting everything up.

"This is just air," Antonio explained to Lewis, tapping the container. "It's the same sort of canister that we use if we have to put on breathing apparatus to go into a burning building."

"Cool!" Lewis replied.

Antonio attached the tubes to a valve at the top of the canister and held his hand out for the squares Lewis was holding. Lewis hastily gave them to him, and Antonio attached them to the other end of the tubes.

Lewis glanced over at the van. All the firefighters except Antonio lay on the floor next to the van's wheels, with piles of wood next to them.

"When the van gets lifted up, they'll put the wood underneath the wheels to make sure it stays steady," Antonio explained. "Ready, Ray?" Antonio asked the RSPCA inspector.

"Yep!" Ray lay down and got ready to shuffle under, right next to the wheel where Bramble was hiding. "Just don't drop the van on me!" he joked.

"Don't worry," Antonio replied. "You're in safe hands."

Antonio placed the lifting bags under the van, and turned the gas canister on. The lifting bags started to inflate like a bouncy castle, getting bigger and bigger.

Lewis felt a hand on his shoulder as Dad pulled him back. "Dad!" he grumbled.

"You can see just as well from over here," Dad told him.

The bags filled up more and more, and slowly the side of the van started to rise. As it did, the firefighters put more and more planks of wood under the van's wheels to keep Bramble and Ray safe.

"OK, here goes," Ray said, passing Antonio the wire animal carrier.

Antonio held the door of the carrier open, and Ray crawled under the van. It was easier now there was much more space. Lewis could hear him murmuring to the little badger as he started to gently free her.

Lewis wished he could see what was going on. *How badly was Bramble hurt?*

What would happen if Ray couldn't get her out? his thoughts raced.

Finally, after what felt like ages, there was a shout from under the van. "Got her!" Ray called, his voice muffled.

"Yes!" Lewis cheered. He and Dad grinned at each other.

"Coming out!" Ray shouted. He shuffled out, feet first. Lewis bent down so he could watch, looking out for a glimpse of the little cub. Antonio held out the carrier as Ray appeared out from under the van, a little black and white bundle cradled in his arms.

"There now, that wasn't so bad, was it?" Ray muttered to Bramble, stroking her reassuringly.

Lewis grinned as he saw her properly. She was a bit mucky from being under the van, but Lewis could see her grey

body and her stripy face. She was only
little, about the size of a cat, but she
was really strong, and she wriggled and
squirmed in Ray's arms.

"You were right, Lewis, she is a girl,"
Ray smiled. "I'd say she's about four months
old." Ray shifted her in his arms as he tried
to put her in the carrier. But just as he was
about to place her inside, Bramble squirmed,
and jumped right out of his hands!

"Stop that badger!" Ray cried.

Lewis gasped as he watched Bramble limping along as fast as she could. She was running straight towards him!

As Bramble ran over to him, Lewis stepped in the way, blocking her path. Bramble raced over to the wall at the side of the road and stopped, looking up at Lewis. "It's OK," Lewis said softly.

"Good lad!" Ray called, running over with the carrier. "Just keep her there for one second."

Lewis spread his arms out wide, making sure she couldn't get past him. He couldn't believe he was seeing her so close. Her grey fur was rough and wiry, a bit like Alfie's, but the black and white stripes on her face were soft and fluffy, and she had white tufts on her little round ears. She was holding her injured leg out awkwardly, and Lewis could see dried blood matting her fur.

Bramble shrank back against the wall nervously. One of her paws scraped against the wall, and Lewis could see that the pads underneath were like a little foot, with five toes and strong claws for digging.

"Careful, Lewis. Don't get too close. She could bite!" Dad said, sounding alarmed.

Bramble turned her nose towards Lewis's leg, but she just sniffed him. "It's OK," Lewis said softly as she trembled.

He knew she was scared, and that scared animals sometimes bit humans that were trying to help them, but somehow he knew Bramble wouldn't hurt him.

"Don't be frightened, Bramble," he soothed, trying to make his voice as calm as possible. "We're trying to help you."

Ray arrived and gently grabbed her, picking her up and putting her safely in the carrier. As Ray shut the carrier's wire door, Lewis let out a deep breath.

"Well done, Lewis!" Antonio said, clapping him on the back. "We might have had to rescue her all over again if it wasn't for you."

"Phew!" Ray said, mopping his forehead. "Thank goodness you were here, Lewis."

Lewis felt his face flush. He just wanted Bramble to be OK. As the firefighters deflated the lifting bags and started packing up their stuff, he went with Ray back over to the RSPCA van.

Bramble was moving about in the carrier. As Ray put her in the back of the van, she looked up at Lewis sadly.

"Don't worry," he told her softly. "You're going to a nice place, and they're going to help your leg get better. Then you can go home, I promise."

Bramble wrinkled her nose like she understood. Then she curled up at the very back of the carrier.

As Ray shut the van, all the firefighters cheered.

"Thanks for all your help, Lewis." Ray said. "You've got a real way with animals."

Lewis grinned with pride.

"Right, I'd better get her back to the centre to have that leg looked at," Ray said.

The firefighters were ready to go as well. One by one, they all came and shook Dad and Ray's hands, clapped Lewis on the back, then climbed into the fire truck.

"Bye, Lewis!" Antonio started the engine, then flashed the lights and sirens.

"Cool!" Lewis grinned.

Antonio waved and gave him a thumbs up,

then switched off the lights and drove off down the lane.

"Goodbye!" Ray said as he got into the van. "And thanks again. Let me know if you ever want a job!"

Dad came and put his arm around Lewis's shoulders as they waved goodbye and watched the RSPCA van drive away. "Well," Dad said as it disappeared around the corner. "What an adventure!" But Lewis couldn't stop thinking about the little badger.

"You know she's going to the best place, right?" Dad told him, giving his shoulder a squeeze.

Lewis nodded sadly.

"Come on, you did a brilliant thing. You saved her life," Dad told him. "And it's an amazing adventure to tell people about. Not everyone gets to help the

RSPCA and the fire brigade all in one morning!"

"I bet Granddad would love to hear about it!" Lewis said, feeling a spark of excitement.

"I bet he would," Dad agreed. "Tell you what, we'll give him a call and see if he wants to have dinner with us tonight, and you can tell him all about it." Dad looked at his watch. "But before then, we've just got time—"

"For what?" Lewis asked as Dad hurried him to the car.

"To get that game!" Dad grinned. "Come on!"

4

Woof, woof, WOOF!

"Hi, Alfie!" Lewis called as he saw the blurry shape of Granddad's dog through the glass door. Granddad arrived after him, then opened the door and his arms wide.

"Lewis!" he grinned. "Come on in."

"Dad's gone to get fish and chips,"
Lewis explained as he followed Granddad
back into his sitting room.

"My favourite!" Granddad said, sitting
back in his chair. "Now, how's my best
grandson?"

"I'm good!" Lewis took his usual
seat on Granddad's footstool, and Alfie
flopped down next to him, waiting for a
stroke. Lewis petted his soft fur and the
greyhound nuzzled into his hand, nudging
him with his long nose. Lewis stroked all
along his nose and tickled him behind the
ears, just the way he liked it, and Alfie's
long tail wagged happily.

Lewis grinned as he looked around.
Granddad's front room had been the
same for as long as he could remember.
The wallpaper was old-fashioned and

faded and a bit peely in places. Dad had offered to redecorate it a million times, but Granddad always said it was just the way he liked it. The fireplace was covered in photos – black and white ones of Granddad and Grandma on their wedding day, Granddad looking young in his Navy uniform, and a big one in the middle of Lewis grinning in his school uniform.

Woof! Alfie sat up, his ears pricked up.

"It's only Dad with the food." Lewis gave him a reassuring pat.

"Go and let him in, Lewis." Granddad waved towards the door. "Saves my old legs getting up again."

"Yeah, right," Lewis laughed. Granddad was always racing around. He walked miles with Alfie every day and he could still beat Lewis at ping-pong. He only ever acted like an old man when there was something he didn't want to do!

Lewis opened the front door and Dad came in, carrying steaming, delicious-smelling takeaway bags.

"Can you go and set the table, Lewis?" Dad asked him.

"Don't bother!" Granddad called. "We'll have it out of the paper, for a treat. Fish and chips tastes better if you eat it with your fingers," he said to Lewis with a wink.

Dad frowned and looked down at his clothes, and Lewis could tell he was worried about getting messy.

"Come on, Dad," Lewis told him. "I want to tell Granddad all about the badger."

Alfie sat at Granddad's feet, looking up at the dinner hungrily. As Lewis munched, he explained about finding Bramble, calling the RSPCA, and the fire engine coming.

"And then she wriggled away from Ray and ran right over to me!" he said proudly. "Ray said if I hadn't been there they'd never have caught her."

"Well, that's brilliant," Granddad grinned. "There's not many people that can say they've saved a badger. I used to do lots of badger watching with your grandma before your dad was born. But I haven't been for years."

"Badger watching?" Lewis asked.

"Yes," Granddad smiled. "When I was home on leave from the Navy we would go down into Brock Wood at dusk, and wait outside the badgers' sett. That's what a badger's house is called," Granddad explained. "You'd sit there so quietly, hardly breathing, just looking at this mound with a load of holes in it. You'd wait and wait until it was dark and you were certain there was nothing there, then all of a sudden you'd see these little noses poking out."

"Bramble had a really snuffly snout," Lewis said excitedly. "It was so cute!"

Granddad nodded knowingly. "Sometimes if you sat in the right place, downwind so they couldn't smell you, whole families would come out and play right in front of you. And we'd see bats flying overhead and foxes and rabbits. The woods come alive at night. Those were the days," he added with a grin.

Lewis smiled. It was so nice thinking about Bramble's life out in the woods, with all her friends.

"I asked your dad if he wanted to come dozens of times when he was a boy," Granddad shook his head, "but he was too busy playing with his computers. You two are very similar, you know."

Lewis didn't think so. It didn't seem like Dad did either, because he nearly choked on his chips.

"I wonder how Bramble's doing at the RSPCA rescue centre?" Lewis thought out loud.

"Did I ever tell you about how I got Alfie?" Granddad asked him.

Alfie's ears pricked up when he heard his name. He had his head on Granddad's lap, and looked up at him adoringly with his chocolatey-brown eyes. Granddad ruffled Alfie's ears and he put out his tongue in a doggy grin.

Lewis slid down to sit next to Alfie and put his arms around him. Granddad had had Alfie for as long as he could

remember, but he'd never heard this story before.

"He used to be a racing greyhound," Granddad explained. "When he was too old to run any more he was badly treated by his owner. The RSPCA got him back to health and looked after him. He got a second chance, thanks to them," Granddad said gruffly.

Woof! Alfie barked like he agreed.

Lewis looked at the happy dog, and shook

his head. He couldn't believe that anyone could ever have been horrible to him.

Alfie rolled over on to his back, his legs up in the air. "Funny old dog!" Lewis laughed. Alfie lifted his head and looked at him, as if he was saying, "Me?"

Lewis sneaked Alfie a chip and the old dog gulped it down happily.

"So, back to school on Monday?" Granddad asked Lewis, making him jump guiltily. "The summer holidays have gone quickly."

"It's OK," Lewis replied. "It'll be good to see all my friends." Then he remembered something. "Oh, I've got a school report to do for Monday."

"Lewis!" Dad exclaimed. "You've had *all summer*, why have you left it so late?"

Lewis shrugged. "I forgot. But maybe that's good – now I can do it on badgers!

Will you help me, Granddad? I've got to stand up in front of the class and talk for five minutes. Maddy's going to do her talk on the new *Ice Storm* game, but if I tell everyone about meeting Bramble, and the fire brigade, and tell them lots of things about how badgers live, my talk will be the best!"

Granddad laughed. "Of course I'll help! Grab a pen and paper and I'll tell you everything I know." He sat forward in his chair, Alfie leaning with him. "A boy badger is called a boar. . ."

". . .and a girl badger is called a sow," Lewis told his class. "Badgers live in small groups in underground homes called setts. They are nocturnal, which means they sleep during the day and get up at night-time." Lewis held up a picture that Dad

had printed for him off the Internet. "I didn't take a picture of my badger," he told the class, "but she looked like this. And that's why badgers are the best!"

Lewis stopped talking, and everyone clapped.

"Well done, Lewis, that was very good. How is your badger doing now?" Mrs Swan asked, her kind face looking concerned.

Lewis shuffled his feet. He wished he knew. He couldn't stop thinking about how Bramble was doing at the centre, wondering if her leg was OK and if she was going back to the wild.

"I don't know," he told her, shaking his head sadly.

"Well," Mrs Swan said brightly, "maybe you could get your parents to call the RSPCA and ask for an update. I'm sure the RSPCA would be happy that you're so interested."

Lewis's face lit up. That was a brilliant idea! "Thanks, Miss," he said as he went to take his seat next to Maddy.

"That was great, Lewis!" Maddy told him. "Bramble sounds so cute. I wish I'd seen her."

"I wish I could see her again," Lewis sighed. "I didn't even get to take a photo of her."

"But you'll always remember her,"

Maddy said. "And I bet she'll remember you!"

Lewis grinned. Maddy always knew the right thing to say. He had lots of friends at school, but Maddy was his best friend.

Maddy was short and skinny, with shoulder-length brown hair that was always in a messy ponytail, and freckles all over her face. When Lewis had met her, he and his friend Tom had laughed when she said she liked computer games – until Maddy had beaten them both at their favourite game. Lewis still felt a bit ashamed for judging Maddy on what she looked like. His mum and dad had always said that the colour of people's skin didn't matter, or whether they were a boy or a girl – it was what they were like inside that counted. Luckily Maddy had forgiven him and they'd been best friends ever since.

A loud noise jolted Lewis out of his daydream.

"Good work, class!" Mrs Swan called as the bell went. "I think because of Lewis's brilliant talk, our project next week should be a piece on our favourite animals. For homework, I'd like you all to write about their habitat – that's where they live – and their diet, as well as what they look like. . ."

When their teacher finished, Maddy jumped up and grabbed her bag. "Come on, Lewis, last one in the playground is it!"

5

Lewis got off the bus and walked down his street, his school bag bumping against the back of his legs. But when he went to unlock the back door, it was already open. Inside, the kitchen table was covered with papers, and there was a delicious smell of cooking.

"Mum?" he called.

"Lewis!" Mum rushed into the kitchen and swept him up in a huge hug. Lewis grinned as he breathed in the smell of cocoa butter and food and Mum all mixed together.

"You're squishing me!" Lewis wriggled out of the hug.

"Stand back and let me look at you!" Mum exclaimed. She pushed Lewis back and looked him up and down. Mum was still dressed in her smart work suit, with heels and a brightly coloured scarf around her neck. Her hair was relaxed straight and cut into a bob. Long earrings swung at her ears and her hands glittered with her rings as she waved them around. "Yep, you've grown," she declared. "You're going to be as tall as your dad."

"I can't have grown in two days!" Lewis laughed. "How come you're back early?"

"The conference finished sooner than I'd thought it would, so I managed to get an earlier flight back to my boys," Mum explained with a grin. "How was your weekend with Dad? I want to hear all about your adventures. Honestly, I leave you two alone for one weekend, and all this exciting stuff happens!"

Mum started sorting out her papers while Lewis explained all about the badger. When Lewis told her about Mrs Swan's idea to phone the RSPCA, she jumped up excitedly. "What a good idea! We'll give them a call now."

As she picked up the phone, Dad walked in the door. "Surprise!" Mum grinned, flinging her arms around him.

"Hello!" Dad put his bag down and whirled Mum around until she laughed. "This is a surprise!"

"What are you doing home already?" Mum asked, looking at her watch.

Lewis felt just as confused as Mum sounded. Dad *always* worked late. He was

never normally home before eight o'clock, and sometimes he didn't get back until after Lewis went to bed. Lewis always lay awake until he heard the click of Dad's key in the door, and his parents' voices murmuring and laughing as they chatted about their days.

"I didn't want Lewis to be home on his own," Dad explained.

"I would have been OK," Lewis

protested. He'd been getting the bus to school on his own for ages, and letting himself in if he got back before Mum finished work.

"I know." Dad ruffled Lewis's hair. "But it's nicer to have company. I thought we could try out your new game."

Lewis brightened up. He couldn't believe Dad wanted to play with him. "OK!" he agreed.

"Oooh, this is lovely," Mum grinned. "We can have a nice family dinner. The food at the conference was terrible." She started bustling about with the pans on the hob. "We were just about to call the RSPCA to find out how Lewis's badger is," she told Dad.

"Oh, I spoke to them earlier," Dad said awkwardly.

"What? How's Bramble?" Lewis almost

leaped out of his chair. *Why had Dad phoned the RSPCA without him?*

"They said she's recovering really nicely," Dad told them. "She's had to have staples put in her leg—"

"Staples?" Lewis interrupted. "Like the ones we use at school?"

"Yes, sort of," Dad explained. "They're just like stitches, they close the wound so it can heal. I think they use staples because they're quicker to put in. She'll be released back into the wild in a few weeks."

Lewis couldn't help feeling sad that he hadn't got to talk to the RSPCA people. "Can we call them again?" he asked. "I wanted to see if she's OK. I thought they could take a picture of her for me."

"Not now," Dad said vaguely. "They've got an awful lot of animals to look after, you know. Maybe we can give them a call tomorrow."

"But, Dad—" Lewis protested.

"I said no," Dad said firmly. "Come on, let's have a nice dinner."

Lewis couldn't believe Dad was being so mean. He knew how much Bramble meant to him.

"How about that game then?" Dad suggested, taking off his tie.

"No, thanks." Lewis pushed back his chair crossly. "I'm going to my room."

He saw Mum and Dad exchanging glances as he stormed out of the kitchen and up the stairs, but Lewis didn't care. He just wanted to know how Bramble was. He wondered about the staples – had they hurt? When Maddy had broken her arm she'd said it itched all the time. He hoped Bramble's leg wasn't itching too much. He thought about her stripy face and nose and felt like he was going to cry. He only wanted to have one photo of her. He bashed his pillow, then turned his Xbox on. *It wasn't fair!*

Alfie streaked past them and hid behind Granddad's legs. "Come out, you daft dog," Granddad chuckled. "It's only a seagull!"

Lewis laughed as the seagull flapped its wings and squawked smugly.

"It was a *big* seagull," he whispered to Alfie, giving him a stroke. Alfie gave a low whine, like he was agreeing.

Granddad bent down and patted the old dog. "It's a good thing Alfie wasn't there when you met your badger – he'd have run a mile!"

Lewis crouched down and stroked

Alfie until his tail started wagging again. They walked down a slope and on to the seafront. Lewis breathed in the fresh air and grinned. He always felt lucky that they lived so close to the sea. Granddad walked Alfie along the beach every day, and Lewis loved coming with them. Sometimes it was grey and the waves pounded against the shore, crashing up against the stony beach and spraying the footpath with droplets of salty water. Other times the water was flat and calm, and so blue that you could hardly see where the sea ended and the sky began. Today it was windy, with bits of paper and crisp packets being whipped along by the breeze, and dozens of brightly coloured windsurfers out on the water.

Lewis and Granddad walked along their usual route, with Alfie trotting next to them.

"How *is* your badger?" Granddad asked. "Have you heard anything?"

"Dad called the RSPCA but he wouldn't let me talk to them," Lewis grumbled, "and I didn't get to ask them to take a picture of her. It's so unfair."

"Now, now, I'm sure your dad had his reasons," Granddad replied. "The important thing is, she's getting better."

"I know." Lewis picked up a stone and threw it out into the sea. "I just can't believe I'm never going to see her again."

"Well, you've always got Alfie," Granddad said with a chuckle.

Alfie ran ahead, following a trail of invisible smells with his nose, but always glancing back to check that Granddad was following him.

"I love Alfie," Lewis grinned as Alfie sniffed a crisp packet, then jumped when the wind blew it. "But I wish I could have a pet of my own."

"You couldn't have kept the badger anyway," Granddad told him. "Wild animals are meant to be out in the wild."

Lewis picked up another stone. "But at least if I had a photo I could have kept that, and shown Maddy and my friends. Now it feels like it never happened."

Lewis threw a stone in the water and it disappeared with a splash. He wiped his wet face with the corner of his sleeve, not knowing if the water was sea spray, or tears.

"I just wish I could see her again. . ." he mumbled sadly.

6

"Don't bring muddy boots into the hall, golden onions hanging on the wall, it's Harvest Time, Harvest Time again!" the class sang.

Lewis hid a grin as he stood onstage with the rest of the choir. The little kids from the baby classes were meant to be doing a dance, but instead they were messing about in their costumes. They were all dressed up as different vegetables, and they looked really funny. He glanced at Maddy, who was playing her recorder in the orchestra. She was laughing out loud as one of the leeks pushed a tomato,

who burst into tears, his face going as red
as his costume.

Mrs Swan rushed over looking flustered,
then stood in front of the stage and
pushed her glasses on top of her head.
"Gather round, class 8A! Thank you for
being so well behaved." She smiled as
another teacher led the little vegetables out
of the hall. "That was really good. I think
we're just about ready for the performance,
which is great, because I want to take

some time off from rehearsing next week to do something really special."

Lewis glanced at Maddy to see if she knew what their teacher meant, but Maddy just shrugged her shoulders.

"Before we go, I have an announcement," Mrs Swan said with a grin. She waved through the glass panel on the hall door, and it opened.

Lewis sat up and stared as his dad walked in. *What was he doing here?* Lewis felt a flash of worry. *Was he in trouble?* But Dad and Mrs Swan were both smiling.

"Next week, we will be going on a class trip!" Mrs Swan announced. "I was so impressed by Lewis's talk about the RSPCA's amazing badger rescue, that I wondered if it would be possible to organize a visit. And the good news is that it was! With Lewis's dad's help, we've set up a class outing to go there on Monday!"

Lewis sat in disbelief as his teacher passed around permission slips. *Dad had helped set up a visit to see Bramble?*

"That's why I didn't want you to talk to the RSPCA the other day," Dad said, coming over to Lewis. "I didn't want to spoil the surprise."

"I can't believe it!" Lewis exclaimed. "Will Bramble still be there?"

"Yes," Dad told him. "And the lady there said that she'll take you and me on a special tour to see her. She can't take the whole class, because having too many people there might scare Bramble, but I've sorted it out with Mrs Swan and I can take you off while everyone else is having their sandwiches."

Lewis could barely speak. *His dad was*

coming on a school trip, and they were going on a special visit to see Bramble! "But what about your work?" he asked.

"I've taken the day off," Dad told him. "I knew you wanted to see your badger again so. . ." he shrugged. "After our adventure, I want to spend more time with you. Father-son time."

Lewis couldn't believe it. Dad *never* had holiday. Now he was taking a day off work just to take him to see Bramble. Lewis jumped off the stage and flung his arms around his dad.

"Whoa!" Dad said in surprise.

"Thanks," Lewis mumbled into Dad's shoulders.

"Right, Class 8A, we're almost there!" Mrs Swan shouted. Lewis and Maddy stopped talking and turned to face her. They were all on the school coach going to the RSPCA rescue centre. Lewis's dad and a couple of the other parents had come along to help, and everyone was very excited. Mrs Swan had given everybody in the class a clipboard, and they all had to write down information about the centre so they could do a project on it when they were back at school. As well as the clipboard, Lewis had Granddad's fancy camera round his neck. Granddad had lent it to him specially. "Make sure you get that picture of your badger," Granddad had told him.

Lewis grinned at Dad as the coach pulled in through the gates. He was *so* excited!

As they got off the coach Lewis looked around excitedly, hoping to catch a glimpse of his first animal. There were two huge buildings, surrounded by paddocks for the animals to run around in. Maddy grabbed his arm and pointed at a lady in RSPCA uniform throwing a ball for a dog in a nearby yard. All around there were people walking dogs, carrying animal baskets and rushing about busily.

"Right, calm down, everyone," Mrs Swan called through the noisy chatter, "and get into pairs."

Maddy grabbed Lewis's arm, and they followed the rest of the class as they walked in a long line up to the door. A friendly-looking lady in an RSPCA uniform was there, along with a familiar-looking man.

"Ray!" Lewis cheered, dragging Maddy and Dad over to see him.

"Hey, Lewis." Ray took off his hat and

plonked it on Lewis's head.

"Are you coming on the tour?" Lewis asked.

Ray shook his head. "I'm on duty. I've just got a call about a sheep that's got its head stuck in a fence, so I'd better go."

"Cool!" Maddy grinned.

"Cathy can tell you everything you need to know," Ray told them. "Have a good visit." He took his hat back and leaned down to speak to Lewis. "I think Bramble has been looking forward to seeing you," he said with a wink.

"Thanks, Ray." Dad, Maddy and Lewis waved him goodbye.

Cathy turned to the class. "I'm Cathy. I'm the education officer and I'm going to give you a tour of the centres we have here. We're lucky enough to have both an animal centre and a wildlife centre." She pointed to the two huge buildings at each side of the courtyard. "They're both run separately, with different people working in each one. In the wildlife centre we work with wild animals that are injured or lost, like the badger you already know about." She smiled at Lewis. "We can have up to eight hundred animals in the wildlife centre in the busy summer months, and about two hundred in the winter."

Lewis stared at the building in amazement. It was hard to believe there were so many different animals inside!

"In the animal centre," Cathy pointed at the other building, "we look after pets and domesticated animals and find new homes for them. Every animal that comes in has different needs. We have room for fifty-seven dogs and seventy-two cats, as well as rabbits, ferrets, guinea pigs and farm animals! We try and limit the contact that the wild animals have with humans, so we're only going to be touring the animal centre today," Cathy announced. "All the animals you'll see in here will be looking for new homes."

"But before you ask, we're not taking any back with us on the coach," Mrs Swan joked.

"Now, if you'd like to follow me. . ."
Cathy led them to the animal centre
and opened the main doors. "Please be
as quiet as possible, as a big noisy group
will scare the animals. And don't put your
fingers in any of the cages – none of our
animals want to hurt you, but they might
think your fingers are a tasty snack."

Cathy led them inside and Lewis felt
his tummy jump with excitement. He
knew he wasn't going to see Bramble
yet, but he was still excited to meet
all the other animals. Cathy swiped her
pass on another door and held it open,
putting her fingers to her lips to hush
them as the class walked inside. Lewis
clamped his mouth shut tight – he
didn't want to frighten the animals. The
rest of the class quietened down too,
whispering to each other and tiptoeing

as they went into a long room filled
with little pens. In each one was a
different dog!

"Awww!" Everyone in Lewis's class
oohed and aahed as they saw them.

Maddy looked at Lewis in excitement.
They went over to the nearest pen and
peered inside. Inside was an old-looking
dog with a white muzzle. As they looked

at her, her tail started wagging excitedly, and she barked hello.

"*Maisie is a ten-year-old Staffordshire Bull Terrier whose owner couldn't look after her any more*," Maddy read out loud from the sign next to the terrier's kennel. "*She's looking for a quiet home where she can be given lots of love.* Oh, I hope you find a home, Maisie!"

Lewis's classmates spread out along the kennels, bending down and peering at the dogs, or making notes about them on their clipboards. Lewis and Maddy walked along, going from pen to pen. There were so many different types of dogs – and they wanted to see them all!

Even Dad seems to be enjoying looking at the animals, Lewis thought as he spotted his dad crouching down by a pen right at the end.

As he saw the little dog his dad was looking at, Lewis's heart jumped. He had white fur with black and brown splodgy patches all over, and a cheeky-looking face. But he didn't look happy at the moment. He was lying with his head on his paws. When Lewis bent down, he looked up and his brown eyes were sad.

"Pip." Lewis read the sign. *Pip was brought in after being hit by a car. His back leg was injured and he'll probably always limp, but he'll make a loving pet.*

"Poor little dog," Dad said.

"Pip," Lewis called gently. Pip looked up at him again, and his tail gave the smallest of wags. *You're just like Badger,* Lewis thought. *She was scared, too.*

Pip looked at him hesitantly. "Here, boy!" Lewis called. Pip's tail gave the tiniest wag.

"Come on," Lewis said. Pip came over to him, limping on his back leg. He came right up to the wire and sniffed at Lewis's hand. "Good boy!" Lewis said, and Pip's tail started wagging again, fast this time. Lewis wished he could stroke him. He was such a lovely dog. . .

"No," Dad interrupted his thoughts. "I've seen that look on your face before, when you want a video game. We're not getting a dog."

Lewis turned indignantly. "I didn't ask

for one!" But his heart sank a bit. For a second there, when he'd seen Dad looking at Pip, he'd dared to hope. . . Lewis gave Pip one last longing look, then turned away. He knew Dad would never let him get a dog. He and Mum had talked about getting one before, but Dad always said no. He said that dogs were a lot of mess and responsibility, and with Mum away so much, he'd end up taking care of it. Lewis had tried to tell him that he'd look after it, but Dad wouldn't listen. Eventually, Mum had given Lewis an apologetic hug and whispered in his ear that they'd get one when he was a bit older.

Lewis tried to hide his disappointment as Cathy took them round all the other enclosures, explaining about the rehoming process and talking to them about being a good pet owner. Finally, Mrs Swan gathered them in a circle. "Right, time for lunch, everyone," she explained. "And Lewis and Mr Riley, Cathy will take you over to see your badger now."

Lewis felt his heart jump again and his bad mood vanished. He was finally going to see Bramble!

"Say hi from me!" Maddy said.

Lewis nodded. He held Granddad's camera tightly as he and Dad followed Cathy out of the animal rehoming centre and across the yard. The wildlife centre was an even bigger building. Dad chatted with Cathy as they went, but Lewis was too nervous to talk.

"What kind of animals do you have in here?" Dad asked.

"A lot of birds – our cleaning technique is used all over the world to help birds caught in oil spills," Cathy told him. "We get foxes and hedgehogs, too, that have injured themselves, or have eaten something they shouldn't have. A lot of animals get hurt by the rubbish that people carelessly throw away. Once we had some baby deer that we had to bottle-feed after their mother died. And," she added with a grin, "we have the occasional badger. Although I've never seen one as cute as yours. We think she's about four months old. She's going to make a full recovery, thanks to you." She grinned at Lewis again.

Cathy swiped her card to open the door and led them through to a big room. It was similar to the pens in the animal rescue centre, but here the enclosures were all different shapes and sizes. It was a lot quieter, and Lewis could feel his heart beating so loudly he was sure Dad and Cathy could hear it.

Cathy led them over to a door with a metal shutter at the top. She pulled the shutter open so Lewis and Dad could see through a glass window. There, curled up in a ball, was a tiny black and white shape. Bramble!

7

Lewis stared at the familiar stripy face in excitement. "Hi, Bramble," he called softly.

Bramble was sleeping on a soft bed in the corner of her pen, but when she heard Lewis's voice she lifted up her head and looked straight at him.

Lewis remembered that Ray had said badgers were nocturnal, sleeping all day and waking up at night. "Sorry to wake you up," Lewis said. Bramble gave a big yawn, showing her teeth and little pink tongue. Then she got up and stretched.

"Here, you can put some food down

for her if you like." Cathy opened the door and gave Lewis a Tupperware box full of peanuts. "Just don't get too close."

Lewis crouched down in the doorway and grinned at the baby badger. "Do you want some treats?" he asked. As soon as she saw the peanuts she got up, sniffing curiously. Lewis took a handful of peanuts and gently threw them over to her. Bramble snuffled after them as they fell

and gobbled them up one by one. Then she looked up at him like she was asking for more.

"Peanuts are her favourite," Cathy told him. As the little badger sniffed after more food, Lewis caught a glimpse of the silver staples in her injured back leg. "She's not limping much at all," he said.

"No," Cathy agreed, "she's healing really well. But it was a deep wound, and if she'd been left in the wild, I don't know if she'd have been OK. She could have easily caught an infection, or become too weak to look for food."

"You saved her life, Lewis," Dad said.

Lewis looked at the little badger as she happily snuffled about, and felt a thrill of pride. "Me, and you, and Ray, and Angelo and his firefighters, and everyone here."

Dad gave him a proud look.

"Can you take our picture, Dad?" Lewis asked.

"I'll take it," Cathy offered. "Then all three of you can be in it."

"Or would you rather it was just you and Bramble?" Dad asked, glancing at Lewis.

Lewis shook his head. "You should be in it too, Dad," he said, thinking about everything Dad had done to organize this trip. "Thanks, Cathy."

"We try not to touch wild animals too much," Cathy told them. "But if you sit down there I think I can get all three of you in the picture." Cathy pointed to the doorway. Lewis sat down and Dad squashed in next to him.

Cathy crouched in front of them, angling the camera so she could get Dad and Lewis in the picture, with Bramble in the background.

"Smile, Bramble!" Lewis said.

Bramble gave a huge yawn, then she plonked down on her bum and scratched her ear with her back leg, just like a dog! Then she reached up to sniff at Lewis's coat with her long stripy nose.

Lewis and Dad laughed and smiled and Cathy clicked the camera again and again.

"You've got some lovely photos there" she told them as she came over. "She really seems to like you," Cathy grinned. "Do you have any pets?"

"No," Lewis shook his head, "I haven't got any."

"Oh, that's a shame." Cathy gave a shrug. "Well, there are lots here that need a good home. There are some that I'd love to take myself, but I've already got two dogs, three cats and a parrot!"

Dad and Lewis laughed. Lewis couldn't imagine having so many pets, but then he guessed anyone who worked at the RSPCA would really love animals. Cathy gave the camera back and Dad and Lewis scrolled through the pictures. There were some brilliant photos of them with Bramble, and the one where she was sniffing Lewis's coat looked almost like she was giving him a little snuffly kiss!

Lewis hugged the camera to his chest. He knew Bramble had to go back to the wild, but he was so sad he'd never see her again. At least now he had a picture that would last for ever.

"You know, we have regular badger watches in the area where Bramble's being released," Cathy said, giving him a handful of leaflets. "So even once she's back out in the wild you could go and visit her. Badgers are very territorial, so it's likely that she'll stay in the same sett all her life. We've done some investigating and we think we know which one her sett is. It's next to a big clearing, only a little way away from the road where you found her. If you come badger watching, I'm sure your guide will point it out."

"Can I, Dad?" Lewis asked.

"Of course!" Dad agreed.

"That'd be brilliant!" Lewis grinned. "You hear that, Bramble? I'll see you again after all!"

Bramble looked up at him, her beady eyes bright, then she gave another enormous yawn. Lewis and Dad both laughed.

Lewis bent down and gave her a little wave before Cathy shut the door. "Next time I see you, you'll be wide awake, back in the woods with all your friends!"

"How was she?" Maddy asked as Lewis and Dad rejoined the group.

"So good!" Lewis said happily. He scrolled through the pictures again to show Maddy.

"She's gorgeous!" Maddy squealed.

"She's going back to the wild but I'm

going to go badger watching and see her then," Lewis said excitedly.

"Oh, wow!" Maddy grinned. "That sounds amazing!"

Mrs Swan clapped her hands. "Right, class, it's almost time to leave, so finish up your lunches and go and say goodbye to your favourite animals!" she smiled.

Lewis had already seen his favourite animal – but there *was* one that he'd like to see again.

"Come on." He grabbed Maddy's arm.

"Lewis, you haven't had your sandwiches yet!" Dad called as they raced away.

"I'll eat them on the coach," Lewis yelled back.

"Half the class are going to go home and beg their parents for a pet," Dad said to Mrs Swan.

"I know," she laughed, "the RSPCA

should do more school trips – they'd find the perfect families for all their animals to be adopted in no time!"

Lewis dragged Maddy down past all the enclosures until they reached the little black and brown dog.

"Pip!" Lewis called. Pip jumped up and gave a surprised bark, as if he was saying, "You've come back!"

Lewis and Maddy grinned as Pip limped over to the door excitedly.

"You should adopt him!" Maddy said. "Pip needs a home and a family, and you need him!"

Lewis looked at Pip and shook his head sadly. It was no good him even thinking about it, Dad would never let him have a pet.

"I'd never be allowed," he said. "But you're going to find a good home, Pip, I know it."

He crouched down and looked into the puppy's chocolatey-brown eyes. Pip put his head on one side and stared back at him, like he understood every word.

"Bye, Pip," he said. "I hope the right person comes for you soon," Lewis whispered as he turned away.

He and Maddy went back to the

coach, and Lewis shrugged off the sadness. Nothing was going to make him sad today. He'd got to see Bramble again *and* he was going to go badger watching!

8

Lewis pulled on a dark T-shirt and hopped about in excitement. It was finally time for the badger watch! As soon as he'd told Granddad about the trip, he'd volunteered to go with him. He was really excited about going out in the woods again – and about finally meeting Lewis's badger.

Lewis looked again at the letter the RSPCA had sent him.

Dear Lewis,

RE: Badger Watch, Friday, 8.00–9.30 p.m.

The night begins at 8 p.m. when there will be a chance to learn a little about our stripy night-time neighbours from our education officer, Jonathan, who will be your guide for the evening.

At dusk, just as it's starting to get dark, we'll set off to the badger watching site in Brock Wood.

Badgers have a very good sense of smell so it is best not to wear perfume, aftershave or hairspray, as this might keep the badgers away.

Wear warm clothes as it can get a bit chilly out there and also boots or wellies as the ground may be muddy. Please ensure that your clothes don't rustle so we can make as little noise as possible!

*Be prepared to be still and quiet whilst
we wait for the badgers to show.*
Happy badger watching!

Lewis put on his coat and flapped his
arms to make sure that it wouldn't rustle
too much. He had wellie boots on, and
his army trousers which had lots of
pockets.

"Have you got your coat on already?"
Mum laughed from the doorway.
"Granddad's not even here yet!"

Lewis grinned. "I was just checking that
I had everything."

"Here, take these." Mum gave him
some snacks and a flask.

"Mum, I'm not going on a picnic!"
Lewis complained.

"Oh, so you don't want hot chocolate?"
Mum waggled the flask.

"Well. . ." Lewis mumbled. *Hot chocolate was his favourite. . .*

"You might be sitting out in the woods for quite a while and I don't want you to get cold and hungry," Mum told him.

"OK, OK," Lewis said. Mum had made him go to bed early last night as well because she was worried about him being up late. Lewis knew he was going to be so excited that he'd have no problems staying awake!

"Can I take some apple for Bramble?" he asked.

"I don't think you're going to be able to feed her," Mum hesitated.

"I know, but I can leave it for her," Lewis said. "Please? And peanuts, they're her favourite."

"OK," Mum agreed.

Just then, there was a bark from outside

and the doorbell went. "Granddad!" Lewis barrelled down the stairs. "Alfie!"

"You're early." Dad appeared out of his office and let them in.

Granddad came in with Alfie trotting behind him. "I couldn't wait," Granddad admitted. "I've been looking forward to this all week."

"Me, too!" Lewis grinned.

"You two are as bad as each other," Mum laughed.

"Now you're sure you'll be OK looking after him?" Granddad asked.

"It's fine, Dad, I can look after Alfie for one night," Dad sighed.

"I was talking to Alfie!" Granddad said, winking at Lewis.

Dad sighed.

Lewis stroked the old dog's ears, and he flopped on to his back, his belly in the air. Lewis stroked his tummy, and Alfie's tail wagged happily.

"Sorry you can't come, Alfie," Lewis said, "but if you were there the badgers wouldn't come out. You'd probably be scared of them anyway!"

"It's a nice clear night," Dad said.

"Just right for badger watching,"

Granddad agreed.

"Why don't you come, Dad?" Lewis asked. "You helped her as much as me. And you organized the visit to the centre."

Dad hesitated. "Well, I do have some work to do. . ."

"Oh, work!" Granddad said. "There's nothing as important as spending time with your boy. I wish I'd been around more when you were Lewis's age, but I was always away with the Navy. Lewis and I are going to remember this night. What are you going to remember if you sit at home on the computer, eh?"

"I'm going to be home anyway," Mum said, "and it doesn't take two of us to look after Alfie. . ."

"Please, Dad," Lewis said. "It'll be father-son time. . ."

"All right," Dad agreed. "It would be nice to see Bramble in her natural habitat."

"Yes!" Lewis cheered. "Now go and find a coat that doesn't rustle."

Dad quickly got ready, and Mum gave Lewis some apple and peanuts. Lewis felt the excitement swirl in his tummy as he put everything in his trouser pockets.

Finally it was time to go. Alfie jumped to his feet as Granddad opened the door to leave.

"Stay," Granddad told him. Alfie gave a soft whine.

"Come on, Alfie," Mum said. "I've got a special snack for you in the kitchen." She held up a doggy treat, and Alfie gave an excited bark.

While Alfie rushed into the kitchen to enjoy his snack, Lewis, Dad and Granddad sneaked out of the front door.

Granddad put the radio on as he drove.
It was just getting dark on the country
roads, and the sky was streaked with pink
as the sun set.

"Dusk is the funny time of day when
it's just getting dark," Granddad explained
to Lewis. "Lots of nocturnal animals come
out now to look for food. It might be
dinner time for us, but it's breakfast for
them!"

Lewis stared out of the window as they
drove along the seaside and up to Brock
Wood. He'd been there lots of times on
walks with Granddad and Alfie, and with
Mum and Maddy on their bikes, but it all
seemed different in the evening light. It
was mysterious, and completely magical.

"The woods look different in the

dark, don't they?" Dad said, echoing his thoughts.

There was a small group waiting at the entrance to the woods as they parked the car. "Welcome to the badger watching!" a tall man said in a low voice. "I'm Jonathan, and I'm going to try and help you see some badgers! We're very lucky tonight because the wind is blowing towards us, so it won't carry our scent over to the sett. And it's not raining! Not that the badgers mind the wet, but it's not as much fun for us," he said with a grin. "The conditions are looking good, so I think there's a strong chance we'll see some badgers tonight."

Lewis felt a thrill of excitement.

"We're looking out for one badger in particular today," Jonathan told the crowd. "A young female cub called Bramble. She had a nasty accident recently, but she was rescued by one of our watchers, Lewis."

Jonathan gestured to Lewis, and Granddad patted him on the back proudly. Lewis felt his face going hot with embarrassment, but he couldn't help feeling proud.

"Bramble wouldn't be here if it wasn't for his quick thinking," Jonathan

continued. "Her leg healed nicely, and the RSPCA released her back into the wild last week. She'll have a lovely life here with all her badger family. We're going to be watching her sett, so hopefully we'll see her tonight."

Jonathan led them into the wood. It was darker under the trees, and Dad brought out a torch so they could follow the warm yellow circle of light. Dad took Granddad's arm as they crunched through the fallen leaves and stepped over twisted tree trunks and logs. There was the sound of birds singing goodnight, and the smell of woodsmoke in the distance.

Lewis felt like he was in a different world – Bramble's world.

In a clearing, Jonathan stopped and pointed to a large round hole, next to a mound of earth. When Lewis looked, he could see other holes in the ground nearby.

"Is that it?" Lewis asked in amazement. He would never have guessed that the holes were the doors to a badger house.

Jonathan squatted down and pointed to the entrance of the hole. It was neat and tidy, apart from a few bits of dead grass. "See that grass?" he told them in a low voice. "That's bedding. Inside the den there's lots of it to make it nice and cosy."

Jonathan threw a piece of grass in the air to double-check the way the wind was blowing, then showed them all where to sit.

Lewis's tummy jumped with excitement. *Maybe Bramble was down in her sett right now, just waking up!*

Jonathan came over to them and helped them find a space where they could see clearly. "We normally have complete quiet while we're watching the badgers, but if I sit with you I should be able to whisper and tell you a bit more about the badgers as they appear."

"Oh, thank you," Dad said.

Jonathan shook his head. "Everyone at the RSPCA was very impressed with Lewis, so this is the least I can do."

Jonathan got up and gently placed a few piles of peanuts in the middle of clearing, then came back to sit with them.

"Now, we wait," he said with a grin.

9

Lewis stared at the hole in the earth. He hardly dared blink in case he missed something. Beside him, Dad rustled as he moved his leg. "Shh!" Lewis whispered.

Lewis sat as still as he could. His eyes got used to the darkness and the noises of the wood, the wind blowing through the trees, shaking the leaves, and the hooting of an owl nearby. They waited and waited, staring at the little hole for so long that Lewis started to wonder if they were waiting in the wrong place.

Suddenly Dad grabbed Lewis's arm, and pointed to the hole. Lewis snapped his gaze back to it. He couldn't see anything . . . but then there was the tip of a snuffly snout, and flash of white. It was a badger!

Slowly, carefully, the badger poked its head out of the hole and sniffed the air. Lewis held his breath. After a long moment, the badger must have decided

it was safe to come out, and it shuffled out of the sett. It was much too big to be Lewis's badger, but it was still incredible to see it out in the wild. It was followed by another smaller badger. Lewis sat up – but it still wasn't Bramble. Lewis had been sure he'd know her when he saw her, but now he wasn't so sure. All the badgers looked so similar! One by one they walked into the clearing.

"That's Hugo and Betty, the dominant boar and sow." Jonathan whispered so quietly that Lewis could only just hear him. "They're always the first to appear. They'll check there's no danger, and it's OK for everyone to come out."

Hugo stretched and gave a huge yawn. Lewis tried hard not to laugh. The old badger looked just like he felt when he woke up to go to school! Then Hugo started rooting in the earth.

Another badger appeared and went straight over to the peanuts. "That's Barney," Jonathan told them. "He's a bit of a greedy guts, and he always goes straight for the food." Barney ate for ages, his nose snuffling in the pile of peanuts.

Everyone sat silently. Lewis glanced at his family. Dad and Granddad were grinning in amazement. Lewis knew how they felt – he couldn't believe they were seeing the badgers right outside their home. But Lewis couldn't help feeling worried too. *Where was Bramble?* These were all too big. What if this wasn't her sett at all?

His eyes scanned the other holes.

Maybe she'd come out of one of those instead.

"Badgers can see in the dark, but their sense of smell is even better. They follow their noses around the sett," Jonathan whispered.

Another nose was poking out of the hole. Lewis sat forward, hardly daring to breathe. A smaller badger came out of the hole. She had beady black eyes, white tufty ears and a slight limp. It was Bramble!

Lewis watched in delight as Bramble came out of the hole, followed by a couple of other young badgers the same size as her. They must be her brothers and sisters!

"There she is!" Jonathan whispered. "And there are her litter mates, Heather and Humphrey. They're all about four months old."

As Jonathan spoke, Lewis couldn't take
his eyes off Bramble. She nuzzled her
nose into the earth, then Lewis saw her
mouth moving as she happily chomped
on something. Her tail looked even
fluffier than before, and her coat was
shiny and healthy. She seemed completely
at home. Lewis would have loved to have
had her as a pet, but looking at her now,
with her brother and sister, he knew that
this was her home.

Lewis sat back and relaxed as he watched the badgers' antics. He was happy to watch them now that he'd seen Bramble and knew she was safe and sound.

Dad carefully poured the hot chocolate out of the flask and handed Lewis some. He cupped his hands around the warm mug, which felt nice against his cold fingers.

As he sipped the hot chocolate, Hugo started hopping backwards, raking up leaves and grass with his front paws.

"What's he doing?" Lewis whispered to Jonathan as quietly as he could.

"He's collecting extra bedding," Jonathan explained. "It's a cold night tonight, so he's making sure he's got an extra leafy blanket!"

Lewis slurped his hot chocolate and thought about his warm bed at home.

It was so funny to think that badgers
needed blankets, just like he did!

Lewis, Granddad, Dad and Jonathan
watched as the badgers snuffled around.
After a while, Lewis found it easy to
tell the badgers apart. Each of them had
different personalities, just like Lewis and
his friends at school.

Barney tried to eat everyone else's

food, and Hugo told him off with a grumbly growl. Heather liked galloping after her brother and sister, racing and chasing them in circles, making an excited chirping noise, just like she was playing chase!

Humphrey was one of the funniest. He wriggled his bum against the grass, then scratched his face with his back legs, before plonking back down on his bum.

Then suddenly all the badgers looked up. Hugo started sniffing the air, then made a sharp noise.

"Uh-oh," Jonathan said under his breath. "I think the wind's changed direction. They've smelt us." All the badgers sniffed the air and race over to the nearest hole, disappearing back into their sett. All except one. Bramble stood up on her back paws, sniffing the air. Then she turned and looked right at Lewis!

Lewis couldn't breathe as Bramble snuffled closer, sniffing the air.

Next to him, he heard Jonathan gasp as Bramble trotted over to them. Lewis dug into his pocket for the pieces of apple Mum had given him. As gently as he could he tossed the apple over to Bramble.

"Hi, Bramble," he said, as the badger crept closer. "Do you remember me? I remember you!"

The little badger cautiously reached out and nibbled the apple.

Bramble munched up the apple, then looked at Lewis and wriggled her nose. He knew she was saying thank you.

"Goodbye, Bramble," Lewis whispered

as she turned and trotted back to the
burrow. He'd never forget her, but he
knew this was where she belonged.

"That was amazing!" Jonathan gasped
as Bramble disappeared into the sett. "I've
never seen anything like it!"

"She remembered me, didn't she, Dad?"
Lewis turned to where his dad and
Granddad were watching with open mouths.

"She certainly did." Dad shook his
head. "That was incredible."

As the badgers disappeared underground, all the other watchers crowded around Lewis in amazement. They walked back towards the cars chattering excitedly about what they'd just seen. It was completely dark now, but the torchlight bobbed along happily.

"Wasn't it funny when Humphrey scratched his bottom!" one lady said.

"I couldn't believe it when your badger came right up to your grandson," another lady exclaimed to Granddad as they crunched through the leaves.

"He's got a way with animals," Granddad said proudly. "That boy needs a pet!"

"I think you might be right," Dad agreed.

"What?" Lewis spun round so quickly that he almost fell over. "What did you say?"

Dad put his arm around his shoulders as they walked out into the car park. In the yellowy light of the lamp posts, Lewis looked at his dad's face to see if he was serious.

"You and Bramble had a real connection – anyone can see that," Dad continued. "She's a wild creature, but there are other animals you could have, as a pet."

Lewis couldn't believe his ears. "You mean like Pip?" he said, immediately thinking about the little dog he'd met at the Rescue Centre. He'd been like the badger, with an injured leg.

"If you promise to look after him, feed him every day and take him for walks. . ." Dad trailed off.

Lewis looked from Dad to Granddad, who was grinning from ear to ear.

"I will!" Lewis almost yelled in excitement.

"Then yes, if Mum thinks it's OK, I think we can get Pip, if he's the one you want." Dad smiled.

"He is!" Lewis grinned. He knew Mum would say yes, she loved animals as much as he did. "Wait until you see him, Granddad, he's perfect! He's got little floppy ears and he's black and white and brown all over. I think he's a mongrel, but that doesn't matter."

"We'll call the RSPCA first thing tomorrow." Dad grinned.

"YES!" Lewis yelled in delight. Then he hugged Dad again. "Thank you," he said into Dad's shoulder. "Thank you so much."

"There's one condition," Dad said seriously, pushing Lewis away and looking

into his eyes.

Lewis's heart started beating fast. *What
was Dad going to say? Was he going to ruin
this somehow?* Lewis felt his heart sink, but
he nodded his head. He'd do anything to
have Pip.

"That you let me come and walk him
with you," Dad grinned. "Father-son
time. And maybe Father-son-Granddad
time, if we go out with Granddad and
Alfie, too."

Lewis let out a deep breath. "Deal!" he grinned, then hugged Dad all over again.

Dad patted his back. "You're welcome. I love you, Lewis, I hope you know that."

"You too, Dad." Lewis squeezed him again. He glanced up to see Granddad nodding happily. He couldn't believe it. Bramble had helped him get a dog of his very own!

Epilogue

Lewis looked out into the audience as he sang in the harvest play. He couldn't believe how much had happened in the last few weeks. He'd seen Bramble at the RSPCA centre, then gone badger watching . . . and she'd helped him get Pip!

Luckily, Pip had still been at the animal centre when they'd called. A lady from the RSPCA had come round and checked they could give Pip a good home, then they'd adopted him. Lewis still couldn't believe he was lucky enough to have a dog of his own.

Lewis searched the audience, and grinned when he spotted Mum. She was sat next to Granddad, with a big smile on her face and tears rolling down her cheeks. Lewis rolled his eyes at her as he sang and made her laugh. Granddad gave him a thumbs up. Maddy's mum and big brother were there, too, although Lewis was pretty certain that Stephen had his earphones in.

But where was Dad? Lewis felt a surge of disappointment. Dad had missed lots of school events before, because he'd been working, but Lewis had thought things were different now. They'd been doing so many father-son things recently . . . Lewis had just hoped that he'd be there.

As the song finished the audience burst into applause and Lewis and the rest of his class gave a bow.

Lewis hurried down from the stage and went to meet his family. "Mum! Gerroff!" Lewis cried as she smothered him in a huge hug.

Just then he heard a familiar bark. Pip! He looked up and saw Dad standing with Pip and Alfie at the very back of the hall. Lewis ran over to them and bent down to stroke Pip, who jumped up and licked his face excitedly.

"Good boy," Lewis laughed. He stroked Pip's velvety ears and grinned.

"I snuck in at the back so Pip and Alfie could watch too," Dad smiled, his blue eyes twinkling. "They thought you were brilliant."

Woof! Pip agreed.

"You came!" Lewis smiled at Dad.

"I wouldn't have missed it for the world," Dad gave him a hug. Pip jumped around their feet excitedly, tangling them up in his lead. "Come on," Dad laughed, leading them over to where Mum and Granddad were waiting. "We've just got time to take these two for a walk before the badger watching tonight."

Lewis nodded. He was so excited about seeing Bramble again. He'd bought some peanuts for her out of his own pocket money, to say a special thank you to her for helping him get Pip. As Lewis thought about the little badger he felt a thrill of happiness. *He'd rescued Bramble, but she'd rescued him and Dad, too.*

The Real-Life Rescue

Although the characters and animals in Lewis's story are fictional, they are based on a real-life rescue in which an injured badger got stuck under a van.

RSPCA Inspector Steve Wickham was called after a young female badger was spotted by a member of the public, who feared she had fallen from the cliff above and broken her leg. But by the time Inspector Wickham arrived, the badger had crawled under a van and hidden beneath the wheel suspension.

Inspector Wickham said: "She was looking for somewhere to hide, and as badgers are nocturnal, I suppose she picked underneath the van as a hiding place because it was dark. If we hadn't spotted her, she could potentially have been stuck there as the van drove off. As it was, she was well and truly caught in the mechanics of the car, and no amount of coaxing was going to get this girl away from her cubby hole."

Eventually, Inspector Wickham was forced to call in the help of East Sussex Fire and Rescue, who lifted up the van and freed the badger.

She was checked by a vet and found to be healthy, and so was returned to the wild.

A poorly baby badger and an adult badger
receive treatment at an RSPCA centre

Facts About Badgers

- Adult male badgers are called "boars".

- Adult female badgers are called "sows".

- Baby badgers are called "cubs".

- Badgers live below ground in deep burrows known as "setts".

- They are mostly nocturnal (active at night).

- Most badgers in Britain live in groups of between five and twelve.

- Badgers feed mainly on earthworms, but they will also eat insects, rodents, rabbits, cereals, fruits and bulbs.

Based on a real-life animal rescue

RSPCA

Bunny
Needs a Friend

Buying this book helps the RSPCA save animals' lives

Take a sneak peek at
another exciting story based
on a real–life animal rescue!

"Hey, wait for me!" called Sarah, pedalling her bike fast to catch up with her dad and big sister, Zoe. It was a beautiful spring day and Sarah had been distracted by the young lambs in the fields and the

flowers on the verges. Bright sunlight streamed through the trees, making her blink as she approached the others. They had stopped by a gate and Dad was leaning against it, pretending to be asleep.

"I wasn't *that* slow," said Sarah as she pulled up. She exchanged a glance with Zoe and both girls reached out to tickle Dad, who opened his eyes and held up his hands in protest.

"Argh, not the four-armed Tickle Monster! Nooooo!" He rode away quickly, with the girls in hot pursuit, laughing. It was their first family bike ride of the year and it felt fantastic to be cycling along the country lanes near their home. Sarah loved her new red bike, with its sparkly mudguards, shiny silver bell and streamers on the handles – a special present from her family for her ninth birthday. Riding it felt like flying!

Both Sarah and her sister enjoyed doing sporting activities with Dad, who always made every expedition fun. Mum was a bit wobbly on a bike, so was happy to have some quiet time at home, where she would be tucked away in her office, writing the next chapter of her new crime novel.

Sarah noticed that Dad was waving his arm up and down ahead. It meant something was coming, so she and Zoe kept to the side of the lane and rode slowly. Very soon, they heard a strange noise that seemed to be getting louder. Suddenly, around a corner, they spied the reason. It was a flock of sheep approaching!

Baaaa, bleated the animals as a farmer moved them along the lane with the help of his two collie dogs. Dad

and the girls pulled over on to a grass
verge to let the sheep pass. Sarah tried to
count them as they went by, but got in a
muddle after fifty as they trotted past in a
blur of wool.

"Thank you!" said the farmer, giving
them a cheery wave as he passed. Sarah

watched him open a gate and shepherd
the sheep into the field, with the dogs
rounding up any that wanted to stay
munching grass on the verge. In a matter
of minutes, the sheep were safely on their
new grazing ground, and the farmer was
leaning on the gate, watching them, with
the dogs at his side. Sarah took a picture
of the flock on her phone.

"Come on, daydreamer!" called Dad,
who had set off on his bike again, with
Zoe close behind.

"I'm taking photos for my art project,"
Sarah called back, hurrying to join her
dad and sister. Sarah's teacher, Miss Tate,
had asked everyone to take five pictures
of spring scenes. The best ones would go
up on the noticeboard in the corridor,
and Sarah, who loved art, really hoped
one of hers would be chosen.

"You've given me an idea," said Dad, as Sarah caught them up. "I think this ride should be more educational."

Zoe and Sarah groaned.

"What happened to Sundays being *fun days*, Dad?" asked Zoe.

"Don't worry," said Dad. "I just wondered if you'd both like to make a little cross-country detour. We could follow the cycle track through the woods. See things we wouldn't spot otherwise."

Sarah was excited. It would give her the chance to test out her bike's gears over bumpy ground.

"Yes, please," she replied enthusiastically.

Zoe was already setting off and beckoned for Sarah to follow. "Come on, sis," she said. "Let's set the pace."

"Watch out for tree roots," Dad called after them.

Just up ahead, a post with a bicycle symbol on it pointed left into the woods. Zoe took the lead, and Sarah followed close behind.

The cycle path curved between trees, rose steeply over banks covered with plants, and dropped away towards a small stream. Twigs snapped under their tyres as they rode, and rooks cawed from the tops of tall ash trees as they passed, surprised by the visitors.

Sarah's teeth chattered together as she cycled after Zoe. Her bike's gears made light work of the uneven ground and Sarah found she was easily able to keep up with her older sister.

Soon they reached a small wooden bridge, and Dad suggested they do a challenge.

"Each of us could make a small boat

out of sticks. We'll put them in the stream, and the first boat to sail under the bridge and appear on the other side will be the winner. We could set a time limit of five minutes. What do you think?" asked Dad.

Sarah thought this would be fun. Zoe, who preferred computer challenges, pulled a face. Both girls dismounted, leaned the bikes against a tree and went in search of sticks. Sarah quickly made a thin twig-boat with a leaf sail. Zoe fashioned a mini canoe out of a branch by peeling back the bark to create pointed ends. Dad made a small, flat raft, held together with reeds that he tied in an artistic knot. When each boat was ready, Dad and the girls crouched by the edge of the stream, holding them above the shallow water.

"Ready?" said Dad. "Get set. Go!"

The boats dropped into the stream, which was moving slowly, bubbling and babbling over stones. Dad's raft sank immediately and he put his head in his hands in pretend shame. Zoe's canoe was heading for the bridge, carried by the gentle current. Sarah's boat grounded for a moment on a reed, then seemed to spin round and sail backwards, catching up with the canoe.

"Come on!" urged Sarah, clapping her hands.

The girls ran on to the bridge, where they cheered their makeshift boats as they disappeared underneath. Seconds later, it was Sarah's boat that appeared, minus its sail, on the other side.

"The winner!" Dad announced. "Well done, you two. Your boats went much further than mine."

"Girl power," said Zoe, giving Sarah a high five. "So, what's the next challenge, Dad?"

"That's easy. We're going to play our favourite travelling game. Can you guess?" he replied, setting off on his bike again.

"I Spy, yay!" said Sarah, who loved word games. "Do you want to go first, Dad?" she asked.

Dad looked pleased. He started to look around for inspiration as they rode along.

"Hmm. I spy with my little eye, something beginning with B." Dad's face didn't give away any clues. He wasn't staring at anything in particular.

"Branch?" suggested Zoe.

"Nope," replied Dad.

"Bee?" Zoe pointed to a large bumble bee, buzzing near Dad's head.

"Where?" asked Dad, crouching low over his handlebars and pretending to be scared. "Not correct, by the way."

"Is it a badger sett?" said Sarah as they passed a large entrance hole in a grassy mound to their left.

"Right answer, eagle eyes. How did you know that?" asked Dad.

"The hole looks like a letter D lying on its side," Sarah answered without hesitation.

"Nature nut," said Zoe, smiling at her sister. "All those animal magazines you read are turning you into a real expert."

"That explains it," said Dad, impressed. "Do you think the badgers are watching us?" he said, looking around suspiciously. "They might be hiding in the trees."

"Badgers don't climb trees," giggled Sarah. "And they're nocturnal, so they'll be asleep during the daytime."

Dad put his finger to his mouth. "Let's be very quiet then," he whispered.

The cycle track was widening, and in a few moments it opened back on to the country lane. Now they were riding on smooth tarmac again, and Sarah felt her arms relax their hold a little. They were a bit stiff after gripping so hard. But it had been worth it. Riding through the woods had been a real adventure, and her confidence on her new bike was growing by the minute.

"Your turn," Zoe reminded her. Sarah was still thinking about the badgers and had almost forgotten the game!

"Let me see.' Sarah looked from side to side and then up the lane, where there was a small lay-by ahead. "Um . . . I spy with my little eye, something beginning with . . . oh my goodness!"

"'Oh my goodness' isn't a letter, silly," said Dad.

But Sarah was applying her brakes and scuffing her feet along the lane to slow herself down. She stopped her bike in the lay-by, propped it against a hedge and knelt by a grassy verge.

Dad and Zoe followed and were soon watching Sarah reach down and try to lift a cardboard box. The box was covered with a lid, which had been sealed shut with thick tape.

"Well spotted, Sarah. I think you're a bit of a detective, like Inspector Wilding in Mum's books," said Dad. "It's good to clear up litter. We can pop it in the recycling when we get home."

"No, Dad. It's not empty. There's something inside. And it's heavy, too." Sarah was having difficulty picking it up.

Dad bent forward and held the box so that Sarah could unstick the tape and remove the lid. As she did so, she let out a surprised gasp. Dad's eyebrows furrowed in disbelief and Zoe's mouth opened in a silent *Oh*.

The sight that greeted them was something so unexpected, they were lost for words. Out of the box popped a pair of long black fluffy ears, followed by a

black and white furry face, bright eyes
and twitching whiskers. The face looked
at each of them in turn, then disappeared
again nervously. Sarah peered inside the
box, astonished to see a small creature
trying to hunch down and hide itself.

"It's a bunny!" she exclaimed quietly,
eyes wide with amazement.

Join the RSPCA!

You'll receive:

- **six issues of *animal action* magazine**
- **a brilliant welcome pack**
- **a FAB joining gift**
- **and a FREE gift with every issue.**

Go to: **www.rspca.org.uk/theclub**

Ask an adult to call:
0300 123 0346 and pay by debit/credit card.

ALL FOR £15!
(£22 OVERSEAS)

RSPCA, Wilberforce Way, Southwater, Horsham, West Sussex RH13 9RS
The RSPCA helps animals in England and Wales. Registered charity no. 219099

For more information on the Animal Action Club check out: www.rspca.org.uk/theden